read 3

DESARROLLE MENTES JOVENES, LEA 3 VECES A LA SEMANA

H-E-B está firmemente comprometido a mejorar la educación en Texas y ha apoyado a las escuelas de Texas a través del programa de Premios a la Excelencia en la Educación por más de 10 años. En 2011, cuando H-E-B se enteró de que Texas enfrentaba un desafío importante con respecto a la educación de la infancia temprana y la preparación para el jardín de niños, H-E-B comenzó la Campaña de Alfabetización de la Infancia Temprana de Read 3.

Los objetivos de Read 3 son proporcionar un acceso fácil y asequible a los libros para las familias de Texas y alentar a las familias a que lean a sus estudiantes que están en la infancia temprana por al menos tres veces a la semana. Leerle a un niño mejora su alfabetización y cuando la alfabetización de un niño mejora, es más probable que tenga éxito en la escuela, menos probabilidades de abandonarla y más probabilidades de terminar la universidad. Ese es un futuro más brillante para el niño, la familia y para Texas.

Comprométase a leer al menos tres veces por semana a su estudiante que está en la infancia temprana. ¡Tome la promesa de Read 3!

"A, B, C y 1, 2, 3 - La lectura es divertida para mí. Me ayuda a desarrollar mi mente joven. ¡Esta semana me comprometo a leer 3 veces!"

This book belongs to:

_____

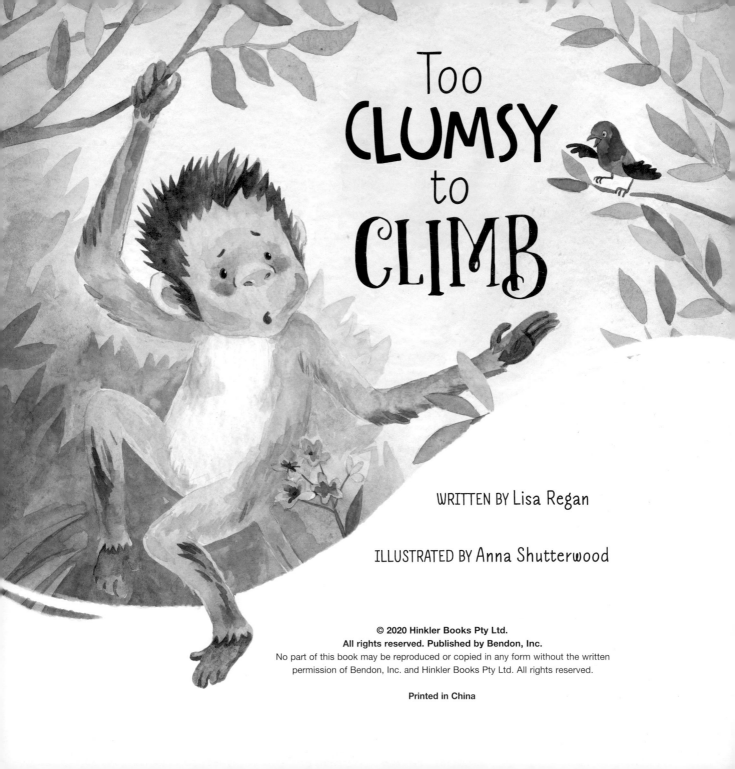

Too CLUMSY to CLIMB

WRITTEN BY Lisa Regan

ILLUSTRATED BY Anna Shutterwood

It's a beautiful morning in the jungle. Mommy Monkey gives Little Monkey a tickle.
"Guess what?" she says. "I think you're ready to learn how to climb by yourself.
Then you'll be able to play in the trees with your cousins!"

Little Monkey wraps his arms tightly around Mommy's neck.
Climbing looks so difficult! How will he manage on his own?
    "Don't worry," Mommy says. "We'll do it together."

First, Mommy and Little Monkey watch their family and friends climbing so he can see how it's done.

"See how they move hand over hand to climb higher? They grip with their feet to push themselves up."

Little Monkey nervously slides off Mommy's back and grasps hold of a branch. "Don't forget to use your tail," she tells him. "It helps you to balance as you change direction. Now you try!"

Little Monkey cautiously reaches above his head
and manages to grab a branch. He smiles
and quickly grabs for another,
but misses and...

WHOOPS!

Luckily, Mommy is waiting below
with open arms. "I've got you," she promises
and gives him a squeeze.

She gently lifts Little Monkey up
and he tries again...

and again...

oh dear!

Little Monkey's eyes glisten with tears. "I'm too clumsy to climb," he sighs.

His mommy dries his eyes and cuddles him close. "Everyone makes mistakes when they're learning. You just need to practice and believe in yourself. Let's take a break and watch your cousins as they climb," she smiles.

Suddenly she puts her finger to her lips. "Shh," she whispers. "Someone is trying to sleep." She points across to Baby Sloth, who is dangling dangerously as she dozes.

Oh no! Baby Sloth starts to slip off the branch.

Luckily, Mommy Sloth is watching close by. Slowly but surely, hand over hand, Mommy Sloth leads Baby Sloth to a safer spot and shows her how to hook her claws safely around a branch.

They close their eyes and settle in for a safe, snuggly sleep.

All of a sudden, a nut bounces off Little Monkey's head. "Hey, watch out!" calls Little Monkey, and he peers upwards into the leaves. Little Macaw peers back.

"Sorry!" he squawks, and picks up another nut in his claws.

Zing! That nut pings out of his grip as well.
This time, Little Monkey sees it coming, and hops out of the way.

"Argh!" squawks the little bird. "I just can't crack this!"

Daddy Macaw hops over
and takes the nut.

He demonstrates
how to steady the nut in his claw,
then how to poke his beak into a
crack in the shell and
rip it apart.

Little Macaw pokes his small beak into a new nut while his Daddy holds it. He bites down hard and eventually manages to make a little hole in the shell. Daddy smiles and helps him open it wider, then holds the nut out for his son to nibble on.

"These nuts are made of tough stuff! It will get easier, I promise," says Daddy.

Encouraged, Little Monkey tries climbing down the tree. Hand over hand, he works his way towards the ground. Suddenly his hands slip...

WAAAAH!

Mommy Monkey grabs his tail just in time, and gently lowers him to the ground. He stands up, only to be knocked over again by a peculiar ball rolling into him.

"Oh, hello!" laughs Little Monkey. It's Little Armadillo!

A pointed nose and bright eyes poke out from the scaly ball. "I'm sorry," Little Armadillo squeaks. "It's this whole curling-up thing. It's a bit tricky! I can roll into a ball, but then I keep tumbling off in the wrong direction!"

Little Monkey watches for a while.
Poor Little Armadillo is right. He still needs
some practice! They laugh as Mommy Armadillo
nudges him back on track.

"You're getting there!" she smiles.
"You'll be brilliant by tomorrow!"

The monkeys spot movement in the long grass. Little Monkey uses his tail to balance as he eagerly lifts himself up onto a low branch to see what's going on.

Barely visible, Little Jaguar creeps up on a butterfly and prepares to pounce.
She squints her eyes and then leaps — but not far enough...

CRASH!

The butterfly flies blissfully off to another flower. "Practice makes perfect," Mommy Jaguar says. "Watch me." Mommy Jaguar fixes her sights on a bright pink flower, pads silently closer, and makes her move.

Bam! Got it!

"Now you try," she purrs.
Little Jaguar copies her mother, leaping from
flower to flower, getting better every time.

"Look at me!" she shouts.
"Rarrrrr!"
Her mother looks on proudly.

Little Monkey pulls at his mommy's arm excitedly. "She's really good now!" he smiles.

Now what's that sound coming from the lake? Little Monkey and his mommy leap into the nearest tree and carefully climb up a branch to take a look.
They see a flurry of feathers and a tangle of long legs.

Poor Little Flamingo
is having terrible trouble standing on
one leg. She just can't keep her balance! She trembles,
teeters and topples, and...

SPLASH!

Daddy Flamingo shows her what to do. He stares straight ahead at a tree on the other side of the lake, then slowly tucks up his leg. Little Flamingo follows his lead.

Little Monkey claps his hands. "Well done!"

Then Daddy Flamingo dabbles his beak in the water to drink. But that's a bit too much for his little one to copy. Splash! Little Flamingo shakes herself dry and laughs.

"Don't worry," Daddy tells her. "You will soon be just as graceful, as long as you keep trying."

"Come now," smiles Mommy Monkey. "It's time to go home." She leaps up through the branches, checking over her shoulder as Little Monkey sticks close behind. Up, up, up they go, until they are back with their family and friends.

Little Monkey hears whooping and clapping. "Look at you, little climber!" calls one cousin. "You did it!" cheers another. Little Monkey looks down at the ground, far below. He climbed here all by himself, without even thinking about it!

Little Monkey feels a warm glow. He has learned to climb and now hc can play with his cousins! Practice really does make perfect.

And climbing really is
the best fun ever!